The Saddest Kitten

Holly Webb

Illustrated by Sophy Williams

LiTTLE TiGER

LONDON

For all the perfect shelter cats
and their amazing owners

STRIPES PUBLISHING LIMITED
An imprint of the Little Tiger Group
1 Coda Studios, 189 Munster Road, London SW6 6AW

A paperback original
First published in Great Britain in 2020

ISBN: 978-1-78895-221-7

MIX
Paper from
responsible sources
FSC
www.fsc.org
FSC® C020471

The Forest Stewardship Council® (FSC®) is a global, not-for-profit
organization dedicated to the promotion of responsible forest management
worldwide. FSC defines standards based on agreed principles for
responsible forest stewardship that are supported by environmental, social,
and economic stakeholders. To learn more, visit www.fsc.org

10 9 8 7 6 5 4 3 2 1

Chapter One

Isla pushed away her plate, leaned her chin on her hand and sighed. "You're so lucky," she told Hailey over the noise of the school dinner hall. "I wish we could adopt a kitten."

"I don't see why you couldn't have one," said Hailey. "You love cats – you always play with Pickle when you come round to mine and he really likes you."

Pickle was Hailey's beautiful black cat and Isla loved making a fuss of him. He even sat on her lap sometimes, when she and Hailey watched TV. Then Isla would sit like a statue, hoping he'd stay.

She shook her head sadly. "I've asked my mum and dad loads of times, but they always say no – Mum thinks Chloe and Sienna are too young. They're only four and she says they'd chase a kitten around too much."

Hailey scraped out the last of her yogurt, looking thoughtful. "I suppose they might. But we've had Pickle since before I was born. I don't think I ever chased him. Maybe Max did? I don't remember it, though."

"Yeah, but Max is sensible," Isla pointed out. "Chloe and Sienna are … not."

"They aren't that bad!" Hailey said, giggling.

"Yesterday they climbed up the shelves in the dining room and tipped a whole bottle of yellow poster paint all over the carpet. Mum says it's never coming out. Now isn't the time to suggest we get a kitten as well." Isla made a face. "So how does it work? Do you go to the animal shelter and check out lots of kittens? That must be so hard. I'm not sure I'd be able to choose!"

"The shelter has a website," Hailey explained. "We looked at pictures of them last night. There are loads – I loved the black and white ones, but they're going to be rehomed in pairs. The shelter likes to do that, so they'll be with a friend. But we only want one kitten because we've already got Pickle."

"Oh, I see. But will they let you have just one?"

"Oh yes. There are three ginger and white kittens, so we could have one of those. And there's a tabby kitten with really long fur – she doesn't have any brothers or sisters. I'm hoping we can have her – she's *so* pretty."

"Oh wow, I love tabby-striped cats!" Isla bounced a little in her chair. "So when are you going to decide?"

"Someone from the shelter's coming round today, Mum said. They have to do a home visit to check that we'll be good cat owners. They want to see if the road outside the house is too busy and that sort of thing."

"But you've already got Pickle," Isla pointed out. "And he's so lovely and friendly. That ought to *prove* you're good cat owners."

Hailey nodded. "I said that! But Mum says they have to make sure." She frowned. "I hope it's OK. I don't think our road's that busy, do you?"

Isla shook her head. Hailey lived

two doors down from her and their road was quite narrow – cars always went down it really slowly. "I've seen Pickle sitting in the middle of the road before," she pointed out. "He glares at the cars and they have to stop and wait for him to move. He couldn't do that if they were going fast."

Hailey grinned. "I know. Mum says she was right to name him Pickle – he's so naughty!"

"Do you think he's going to be OK, having another cat in the house?" Isla asked.

"Of course he will!" Hailey stared at her. "Mum and Dad already had another cat when they first got Pickle – he was fine. And you just said he was lovely and friendly!"

Isla blinked. Hailey sounded almost cross. "Yeah, I know he is, but cats like their own space, don't they? Pickle thinks your house is *his* house. What if he doesn't want another cat to share it?"

"He won't be like that," Hailey said firmly. "He'll love having a kitten around. Mum said it's going to give him a new lease of life – he'll enjoy playing with the kitten and he won't spend the whole day sleeping like he does now."

"Sleeping in the middle of the road," Isla giggled.

That afternoon, after school, Isla and Hailey were going to walk home with

Hailey's mum and her younger brother Max, who was in the year below them. Isla's mum and Hailey's mum took it in turns to do the school run since they lived so close to each other.

Hailey dashed across the playground to find her mum as soon as they were let out and Isla hurried after her.

"Mum! Did the person from the shelter come round today? What did they say?" Hailey demanded, throwing her arms round her mum's middle.

"Hello, sweetheart. Did you have a good day? Hi, Isla." Hailey's mum smiled at her.

"Mum! The cat person! What happened?"

"Well, she said the road was fine and it was good that we had a garden. She

was a bit worried about Pickle, but—
Oh, there's Max!"

Hailey and Isla exchanged worried
glances as Hailey's mum stopped to
wave at Max and then admire the
star sticker on the worksheet he was
showing her.

"What did the lady say about Pickle, Mum?" Hailey broke in eventually as her mum was making sure that Max had brought all of his PE kit home to be washed.

"Oh! Sorry, Hailey. She said sometimes an older cat finds it hard to get used to sharing with a new kitten, but I explained that Pickle is super chilled. How he never fights with any of the other cats in the street and he's very friendly."

"That's what I said to Isla," Hailey agreed, nodding.

"He doesn't even mind that little ginger cat from down the road sitting in our garden," Hailey's mum went on. "So I told her all that and she said in that case he'd probably be fine. But we have to introduce them to each other carefully and give them their own space for the first few days. It was all very sensible."

"So … she said yes? We can have a kitten?" Hailey hugged her mum again and then Max hugged her too.

Isla watched, trying not to feel a little envious. She was glad for Hailey – but Hailey and Max already had Pickle and he was gorgeous! Now they were getting a kitten too? It was hard not to be just a *tiny* bit jealous…

Hailey's mum was laughing. "Yes! I called your dad and we agreed we'd go to the shelter tomorrow morning and have a look."

Hailey nodded eagerly. "I hope no one's adopted that tabby kitten!"

Chapter Two

The tabby kitten padded across the
wooden floor, her ears flickering. She
was very confused. Until today, she
had been sharing a pen with three
ginger and white kittens, a brother and
two sisters. They'd curled up in the
same basket, squabbled over food and
chased each other's tails. There had
been people too, bringing them their

meals and cleaning up the pen, but she hadn't noticed them all that much.

Now everything had changed and she didn't understand what was happening. There were no more ginger and white kittens. She was alone in a big room, with a new bed that smelled strange and a food bowl that seemed to be just for her. She curled up in the clean-smelling bed, feeling very small and very alone.

There was another cat somewhere, though. She was sure of it. She could smell it and, when the people had first brought her into the house in that odd, jolting carrier, she had heard a cat. There had been mewing as it was bundled away into another room.

The little kitten huddled closer to the cushioned side of the bed and stared wide-eyed at the door. The handle was rattling. Someone was coming in!

Two someones – a woman and a girl. They had come to top up her food bowl and bring her fresh water, and then the girl sat down on the floor by her basket and made squeaky noises, gently patting her knees and whispering. The kitten eyed her anxiously.

"Don't scare her, Hailey."

"I'm not! I just wanted to stroke her."

"OK, but you know they said we had

to take it slowly. Besides, we probably smell like Pickle to her. I expect she's confused."

The kitten watched them talk, her eyes darting from person to person. The girl was very close and that worried her, but she did sound gentle. And the food smelled good – it was making her hungry. Cautiously, she sat up and crawled to the edge of the basket.

"Let her get at the food, Hailey. Move back a bit. I think she's nervous about going past you."

The kitten twitched her tail as the girl moved, but she was only backing away so that was all right. She kept watching the girl as she went over to the bowl, gulping down the food with one eye on the people all the time. There was definitely another cat – she could smell it on them. A boy cat who'd lived here a long time, she thought. His scent was everywhere. This was *his* house.

The kitten finished the bowl of food and sipped a little water. She was feeling sleepy now and the girl had been so quiet all the time she was eating. Perhaps it was safe to go and have a look at her? A bit of a sniff?

She padded slowly forwards, keeping her bottom and tail nervously low. She was ready to leap back at once if either of them made any sudden movements. But they didn't. The girl was so still, she was hardly even breathing.

The kitten sniffed at her shoe and then started to climb, slowly and carefully, up on to her foot. The girl felt warm and her trousers were soft. The kitten slumped sideways against her crossed legs and yawned.

Just then the door creaked a little, sliding slowly inwards, and the kitten's eyes widened. What was happening? Who was coming in now?

"Mum! You didn't shut the door!" the girl yelped, leaning protectively over the kitten, reaching for her.

The kitten saw the big hands coming and quivered with fright. She didn't know where to run. Where was safe? She squeaked in dismay and then her fur stood up all over as a huge black cat stalked into the room.

It was him – the one this house belonged to – and he was angry!

His ears were flattened right back, as though he was ready for a fight, and he was hissing loudly.

The kitten tucked her bottlebrush tail right underneath her and scurried in terror for the shelter of her basket – the only safe place she knew. She watched, her heart hammering, as the woman hurried across the room, swept the big black cat up in her arms and carried him out. He was still hissing furiously and the kitten huddled in her basket – even the air felt angry. What was she doing here, in someone else's home?

"Did you get her? Did you choose the tabby kitten? Can I come and see her after school?" Isla asked eagerly as soon as she opened the door to Hailey.

She dragged on her coat and called, "Bye, Mum!"

Isla's mum was watching Sienna and Chloe eat breakfast. Their nursery started later than school and it was a bit much to expect Hailey's mum or dad to take them as well. She hurried out of the kitchen to say goodbye, waving to Hailey's dad at the end of the path. "Have you got your homework folder, Isla?"

"Yup. See you later! Oh, Mum, can I pop in and see Hailey's new kitten on the way home? If that's OK with them? I can ask her dad."

"Yes – but don't be too long. Have a good day!" Her mum straightened Isla's coat – it was tricky to get it on just right sometimes.

"So did you choose the tabby kitten?" Isla asked again as they went to the gate. "I've been thinking about you all weekend. I really wanted to come round yesterday but we were visiting my gran."

"Yes. She's beautiful," Hailey said proudly. "We chose her on Saturday and then went to pick her up that afternoon. Once we'd got food bowls and a basket and things."

"Would it be OK if I came and saw her after school?" Isla said pleadingly.

"That's fine, isn't it, Dad, for Isla to come over later?" Hailey asked. "But can I show her some of the photos on your phone now?"

"Not right this minute," said

Hailey's dad. "Max is already halfway up the road. Let's get to school first and then Isla can look. You must have taken about fifty photos already, so it might take a while!"

Hailey sighed, but her dad just grinned at her and shooed them on. When they got to the school playground, he pulled out his phone and Hailey took it eagerly.

"Oh, she's so gorgeous," Isla murmured as Hailey started to scroll through the photos. The kitten was a tabby, with long silky fur and perfect little white boots on all four paws. "Are you keeping her in the dining room then?" she asked – all the photos seemed to be by chair legs or half under the table.

"Yes – the people at the shelter said it was the best thing to do in the beginning because we already have another cat. We keep Silky in one room—"

"Silky! Is that what you're calling her? Because of her lovely long fur?"

Hailey nodded. "She really is silky," she said, smiling down at the photo on the screen. The kitten was gazing out at them with big blue-green eyes. "Her fur's so soft. She's in the dining room and Pickle's supposed to smell her through the door and get used to her scent and not feel too threatened. Then we'll gradually introduce them to each other until they become friends." Hailey sighed. "That's the plan, anyway."

"Isn't it working?"

"Ummm, not really. Mum forgot to shut the dining-room door on Saturday afternoon – she says it was me but it definitely wasn't! Then Pickle came in while we were trying to get to know Silky and he was furious. He was lashing his tail and hissing – I've never heard him make a noise like that. It was really scary!

Mum had to grab him and take him out or I really think he might have jumped on Silky."

Hailey's nose scrunched up and she frowned. "He scratched Mum as she was carrying him out of the door and he *never* scratches. We're supposed to bring Pickle into the dining room for a few minutes every day. But when we tried it yesterday, Silky ran behind Max's drum kit and wouldn't come out, and Pickle stomped up and down in front of the drums, hissing and spitting like anything."

"It'll be OK, Hailey," her dad said reassuringly. "They just need a little more time. Pickle's ten, you know. He hasn't shared a house with another cat since we had Marmalade, but that was years ago. And then it was Marmalade who was in charge and Pickle was the kitten. He's not sure what's going on but he'll get used to it."

Hailey nodded. "I know. But I don't like seeing him so cross. And I hate it that Silky's so scared. When she can't hear Pickle hissing outside the room, she's really sweet and friendly, but even hearing him sniffing at the door makes her nervous."

"Poor Silky. Poor both of them," Isla said sympathetically.

"I just want them to be friends," Hailey said. "Before Silky came, I imagined them snuggling up together on the sofa, and sleeping in the same basket." She sighed again and handed the phone back to her dad. "But Dad's right. They just need time to get used to each other."

Hailey's dad put the phone back in his pocket. "Don't worry. They'll be curled up together on the sofa in no time."

Isla peered under the table and flicked the piece of string she was holding. She giggled as the little tabby kitten settled into a hunting crouch, her tail swishing from side to side. She watched for a few seconds and then leaped on the string with fierce growls. Silky was so small and bouncy – she could fling herself around like a rubber ball, squirming and wriggling with the string.

"She's so sweet!" Isla whispered to Hailey.

"I know," Hailey said proudly. "I love her – she's really funny."

Hailey's mum edged carefully round the side of the door, obviously trying to stop Pickle getting in. She had a food bowl in her hand and, the moment she put it down on the plastic mat, the kitten danced over to it, the string still trailing round her back paws.

"She's forgotten about it!" Isla giggled.

"Do you two want to come and have some strawberry milk?" Hailey's mum asked. "I got some as a treat."

Isla would have preferred to stay and watch Silky for a bit longer, but it seemed rude to say no, so she followed Hailey and her mum into the kitchen. Pickle was still sitting outside the dining-room door and he tried to sneak in as they came out.

"Come on, Pickle." Hailey's mum scooped him up in her arms. "You can have your tea too." But as soon as she put him down on the kitchen floor by his bowl, Pickle marched straight

back out again and began to pace up
and down by the dining-room door.
The fur on his back was standing up in
spikes, so he looked like a dinosaur.
A hissing, angry black dinosaur cat,
who didn't know what had happened
to his house.

Chapter Three

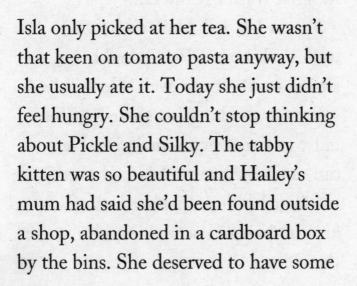

Isla only picked at her tea. She wasn't that keen on tomato pasta anyway, but she usually ate it. Today she just didn't feel hungry. She couldn't stop thinking about Pickle and Silky. The tabby kitten was so beautiful and Hailey's mum had said she'd been found outside a shop, abandoned in a cardboard box by the bins. She deserved to have some

good luck now, after such a sad start.
She needed a lovely home and Hailey's
house would be one, if it wasn't for
Pickle.

It wasn't Pickle's fault, though.
He'd been living with Hailey and her
family for years and years, and now
suddenly everything had changed and
he was just supposed to put up with
it. That wasn't really fair.

When Isla left Hailey's house to
walk back home, Pickle had been
sitting on the front wall. He still had
spiky fur all along his spine and his
tail was twice its normal size. He
did not look happy. Isla had tried
to cheer him up, making lots of
kissy noises and scratching him under
the chin.

He let
her stroke
him, but
he didn't
stand up
and arch
his back and
purr like he
usually did. He just sat
there and twitched his tail grumpily.

I'd be angry and upset too, Isla
thought, *if a new child turned up in my
house without any warning.*

She had been five when Chloe and
Sienna were born. Before they arrived
her mum and dad had talked to her a
lot about new brothers or sisters, and
how she was still special, and how
much they loved her. She'd had ages

to get used to the idea but she still wished she was an only child again sometimes, instead of a big sister. Particularly on days when Sienna and Chloe were being annoying.

Isla had watched Pickle – a hunched patch of darkness on Hailey's garden wall – as she walked the little way down the street to her front gate. He didn't seem to be looking at the birds, or checking out the cars going down the street, like he usually did. He was just staring gloomily at the bricks.

"Eat some more pasta, Isla," Mum said, looking over at her.

Isla sighed and dug her fork in.

"I'm not very hungry," she said a few moments later, stirring the pasta. "Can I go and do my homework?"

Her mum blinked. Usually she had to remind Isla over and over to get her homework done. "I suppose so. You're really not hungry? Are you feeling all right?"

"Yeah… Just worrying about Hailey. Pickle doesn't like the new kitten."

Mum nodded. "Oh dear. Well I'm sure he'll get used to having another cat around soon. Don't fret, Isla."

Isla wandered off upstairs, still miserable. Poor Pickle – what if he *didn't* get used to it? Everyone seemed to think that he would and that he *ought to*. It was almost as if it was his own fault that he was upset and angry.

She scrawled her way through her maths homework, then stuffed it in her backpack and went to change into her pyjamas. Worrying made her tired, Isla decided. She didn't feel like going downstairs to watch TV or play with Chloe and Sienna. She lay down on her bed instead, flicking through an old animal magazine.

If Pickle never decided to be friends with Silky, what would happen then? Isla turned over and pressed her nose into her pillow. Would Hailey's mum and dad keep them both and just let them fight all the time? It would be awful. Pickle was miserable and Silky was scared. Neither of them would be happy.

What could be done about it, though?

Isla turned over on her back and stared up at the ceiling. She couldn't see how it was all going to work out. The only solution was for Silky to go back to the shelter and then she would have been abandoned *twice*.

It wasn't fair.

If Silky belonged to me, Isla thought, biting her lip, *I'd look after her so well. It's not that Hailey's family isn't looking after her – but they thought they would be the perfect home for her and they're just not.*

She shuffled her toes under the duvet, imagining a soft heavy lump of kitten slumped on top of them. She couldn't help it. At her house, there was no sad older cat who needed his own family back, so Silky would be loved and fussed over and petted. Probably fussed over too much…

Isla sighed. That was exactly what Mum and Dad would say – that Chloe and Sienna were too young and not responsible enough. That they wouldn't be able to cope with three children and a cat. Isla had begged so many times.

Over the next few days, Isla kept asking Hailey about Pickle and Silky.

Maybe she went on about it a bit too much because Hailey started to look upset whenever Isla mentioned cats. She definitely tried to change the subject.

"So have you let Silky out of the dining room yet?" Isla asked as they walked back home on Friday afternoon. She'd tried not to talk about the cats all day but she was desperate to know what was happening.

Hailey made a face. "Yes. Mum was working from home yesterday, so she decided it was time."

Isla waited and eventually Hailey added, "Silky's still really scared of Pickle, though."

"Poor kitten." Isla sighed.

"It'll get better," Hailey said firmly. "They'll settle down and one of these days we'll laugh about how they used to fight."

"How's Pickle doing?"

"He keeps lurking about and glaring at Silky until we shoo him away. He's jumped out at her a couple of times, so she just keeps hiding behind the sofa. She tried to climb the curtains to get away from him this morning. Mum wasn't very happy about that."

Then Hailey brightened up. "But guess what? She slept on my bed last night! She was so cute, all curled up."

"Oh!" Isla felt a tight squeeze of jealousy inside her. Just like she'd imagined... Then she frowned. "But I thought Pickle always slept on your bed?"

"Not always," Hailey said defensively. "He often sleeps with Max. And with Mum and Dad sometimes."

Isla nodded. She didn't want to fall out with Hailey. They hardly ever argued. They'd been best friends since they went to the same nursery. Mum had been worried about Isla starting nursery because she thought Isla would find it hard to cope with only one arm, and that the other children might tease her.

When they'd sat down for a drink

of water on that first day, Hailey had looked at Isla's water bottle and said, "Can you open that by yourself?" And Isla had nodded. After that, Hailey never said anything about Isla's arm again and they were just friends.

"Maybe when it's the summer holidays you can help cheer Pickle up and get him used to Silky," she suggested. "There's only a couple more weeks of school."

Hailey brightened up. "Two more weeks!"

Silky blinked and yawned and curled herself tighter into the warm space behind Hailey's knees. It had been raining and the night was chilly for July. The bed was so cosy, even if Hailey did wriggle about. Half asleep, Silky kneaded her paws in and out, almost remembering curling up with her mother. It felt so long ago.

A faint noise out on the landing jolted her wide awake again. Her ears pricked up and her heart began to race. Was it the other cat? She had avoided him for most of the day – he'd been outside a lot and then she had followed Hailey's mum around. The people in the house always grabbed the other cat, or sometimes picked her up to get her out of his way, so she felt safer if she stayed with them.

Silky started to stand up, ready to jump away and hide if he came closer, but Pickle was faster than she was. He surged across the room in the shadows and leaped up on to the bed. Then he smacked hard at the kitten's nose with one huge paw, hissing all the while.

The duvet moved underneath Silky, knocking her off balance as Hailey sat up in shock.

"What's happening? Pickle? Hey!"

Silky staggered backwards, her fur on end, squeaking with fright. She'd been sleeping, that was all! Why was the big cat attacking her?

Pickle smacked her again, this time with his claws out, and Silky felt them scrape across her nose. She flattened her fragile ears back and fluffed up all over, trying to look bigger. Trying to look at least a tiny bit scary.

"Pickle, no!" Hailey yelled. "Leave her alone. Bad cat!" She leaned over, picking Silky up and cuddling her close, pressed up against her nightie.

"Hailey, it's the middle of the night – what are you doing?" Hailey's dad stomped sleepily into her bedroom and flicked on the light. "Oh – it's those cats. I should have known. Right, give me the kitten. She can go back in the dining room, since her bed's still there."

Silky squeaked again, blinking in the light as Hailey's dad grabbed her and marched downstairs. He put her down in her bed quite gently but he shut the door with a bang. The little tabby kitten sat there, wide-eyed and shivering, for a long time.

Chapter Four

"We're going to splash you!" Isla
yelled, and Sienna and Chloe squealed
with delight. It was the first really hot
day of the holidays and Hailey's mum
had let her invite Isla round to play in
their big paddling pool. Then she'd
seen Chloe and Sienna looking envious
and invited them too, and Isla's mum
for a coffee. Hailey and Isla had been

chasing the little ones with water pistols and then gone on to plastic bottles out of the recycling bin, since they held more water. There were puddles all over the grass.

"I think you should all stop and have an ice lolly," said Hailey's mum, coming out with a box. "It's so hot! You look like you need a sit-down. And then probably more sun cream."

Isla and Hailey flopped down on the bench outside the back door to eat their lollies. It was so hot that the patio felt like it was burning Isla's feet. She drew them up on to the bench and looked at Hailey. "What are you staring at the bushes for?" she asked, trying to see where Hailey was looking.

"We've started letting Silky go out in the garden," Hailey told her. "She loves it. I was just seeing if I could spot her."

"Oh! I thought she must be asleep on your bed or something!" Isla said, looking around eagerly. "I didn't realize she was out here too."

"She likes the garden on the other side of our fence," Hayley explained. "She creeps underneath it. They've got a pond with fish in – she sits and watches them."

Isla smiled, imagining it. A pond must be a bit like kitten TV. After that, she kept an eye out in case Silky popped back under the fence but there was no sign of the little kitten.

Isla's mum took Sienna and Chloe home after a bit – she said the big girls needed some time to themselves – and Hailey and Isla flopped down on to a picnic rug. They were chatting when Isla suddenly froze – she'd caught a movement in the bushes by the fence. "Is that Silky coming back?" she whispered to Hailey

"Yes! Oh look! She's spotted a butterfly. She loves trying to chase them."

Isla watched, holding her hand over
her mouth to stop herself
from laughing out loud.
Silky was bounding
about after the peacock
butterfly, even hopping
up on to her hind paws to
try and catch it. But it kept
swooping away, just out
of reach.

After one really
acrobatic jump, the
butterfly soared over Silky's head, and
she tried to lean back and snatch it out
of the air. Hailey and Isla caught their
breath as the tabby kitten teetered
and fell over backwards. She squirmed
upright again at once, looking
disgruntled.

"Awww. Is she OK?" Isla eyed Silky worriedly. She was washing her ears very thoroughly – maybe they hurt?

Hailey grinned. "She's fine. Cats do that when they're embarrassed. She's pretending it didn't happen!"

"She looks as though she's enjoying the garden… So are things a bit better with her and Pickle?" Isla didn't look at Hailey as she said it – she didn't want to keep going on and on.

"Ye-e-e-es. I suppose so." Hailey sounded doubtful.

Isla waited.

"It's better now that Silky can go outside. But Pickle still hisses at her all the time. And if he comes into a room, then Silky runs out." Hailey fiddled with the daisy chain she was making and sighed. "Actually, it's horrible."

"Oh… Well, at least Silky's not still shut in the dining room. That's good, isn't it?" Isla said.

"Yeah…"

"Um, maybe we can do this again tomorrow," Isla suggested, trying to think how to cheer Hailey up. "You could come over to ours. I bet Mum wouldn't mind. I can ask her?"

Hailey shook her head. "I wish I could. But we're going away – it's my gran's seventieth birthday. There's a party and all the family's going to stay in a hotel for the night."

"Oh wow, lucky you!"

"I don't want to go," Hailey said miserably. "I tried to talk to Mum about it but she said we had to. It's been planned for ages and it's Gran's special day."

"But why?" Isla asked, frowning. A night away in a hotel sounded great to her. "It'll be fun. The hotel might even have a proper pool!"

"Silky and Pickle." Hailey looked up at her anxiously. "We've got two special cat feeders with timers on, so Mum says it's OK to leave them because it's only overnight. But they're always fighting! What if they have a big fight while we're away? Silky's already got a scratch on her nose. I don't want to leave them alone together – but I don't want to miss Gran's special birthday either."

Isla stared at the pattern on the rug, trying to think. After the way she'd seen Pickle behaving before, she wouldn't want to leave them overnight either. "Could you put Silky back in the dining room?" she suggested. "I know she probably won't be that happy about it but at least she won't be able to fight with Pickle."

"Yeah, maybe." Hailey nodded. "She'll hate it but you're right – it's better than keeping them together."

Isla jumped up. "Hang on a minute! I've had an idea but I just need to pop home for a second." She darted along Hailey's side path and dashed down the street to her house.

"Mum, are we doing anything tomorrow or Sunday?" she asked hopefully when her mum answered the door.

"I'm not sure. Why?" Her mum sounded cautious, as though she thought Isla might be about to plan a sudden day out, or maybe a huge party.

"Hailey's family are going away because it's her gran's birthday. It's just overnight, but Hailey's worried about leaving Silky and Pickle – you know how they keep fighting. Could I be their cat sitter? Just pop in every few hours and make sure they're OK?"

"I suppose so," Isla's mum said

slowly. "Dad or I would have to go with you but that shouldn't be a problem. We're around most of the weekend. Do you want me to talk to Hailey's mum about it?"

"Yes! Oh thanks, Mum – you're a star! I'll tell Hailey." Isla ran back along the road and flung herself down on the rug. "Mum says yes!"

Hailey looked at her blankly. "Yes to what?"

"Oh! Sorry!" Isla rolled her eyes. "I went to ask her if I could cat sit Pickle and Silky while you're away. I could pop round to your house and check they're OK. Not just at mealtimes, maybe every couple of hours? I can make a fuss of them both and you won't have to worry about them."

Hailey looked hopeful. "Really? Your mum said you could do that?"

"Yes. She says she or Dad would have to come too. I don't really see why but it doesn't matter. As long as I can go."

"That's brilliant." Hailey hugged Isla hard. "You're so clever, thank you!"

The kitten peered out from underneath Hailey's bed. There was a strange feeling in the house this morning. People kept running up and down the stairs and doors were banging. There were bags and boxes in the hallway too. She she had found the trailing end of a string of bunting and pounced on it with fierce growls and sharp claws,

but Hailey's mum had unhooked
her and tucked it away. Then Silky
had climbed all the way up the stairs
to Hailey's room by herself, which
was still quite hard work, but Hailey
seemed too busy to play with her. She
was sitting on the floor with a bag,
putting things in and taking them
out again, and murmuring to herself.
Every so often, she jumped up and ran
to fetch something.

"Pyjamas!" she said, looking over at
Silky under the bed. "I nearly forgot!"

As Hailey rummaged in a drawer,
Silky padded out and sniffed at the
bag. It smelled … interesting. It
smelled of Hailey but of outside too.
She put her paws up on the side and
looked in. Soft clothes, mostly, and a

couple of teddy bears. Hailey was still searching through the drawer and she didn't notice as Silky hopped up on to the bag and then scrambled inside. It was cosy in there and the little kitten felt safe, nestled inside Hailey's clothes, with the top of the bag drawn over her head. She was always on the lookout for places like this – places where she could hide from Pickle.

She yawned and flexed her tiny claws in and out of Hailey's hoodie. She could feel her eyelids closing. So soft, in here…

Silky woke with a squeak when Hailey's pyjamas landed on her head. She sat up, confused and blinking, and wriggled out to look up indignantly at Hailey.

"Oh, Silky, there you are. I'm sorry!" Hailey was laughing as she picked up the little kitten, untangling her from the pyjamas. "It's OK. I didn't mean to squash you. I didn't know you'd jumped in there!" She tickled Silky under her chin and the kitten pointed her nose to the ceiling and purred. That was her favourite place to be scratched.

"You can't come with us. I'm really sorry," Hailey whispered. "But you'll be fine. Isla's going to look after you. And you like Isla, I know you do. She's so excited. She's going to make you a new cat toy – she showed me a picture."

"Hailey! Are you nearly done? We need to get going!"

"Coming, Mum!"

Silky stamped her paws with pleasure as Hailey smoothed one finger gently along her back. "Bye, little one. See you tomorrow afternoon. You'll be OK…"

Silky followed her out on to the landing and watched as Hailey hurried down the stairs with her bag.

"Did you pack your nice shoes?"

"Yes, Mum! You already asked me!"

And they were gone, just like that, when Silky was only halfway down the staircase. She stood there, watching the front door swing shut and listening to the car rumbling away.

The house felt strangely empty and so quiet. Silky wondered where Pickle had gone.

Chapter Five

"Mum – can we go round to Hailey's?
They were leaving mid-morning,
Hailey said, and I promised I'd go and
check on the cats at lunchtime."

Isla's mum looked at her, frowning
a little. "Ummm, not right now, Isla.
Sorry. Dad's gone to the supermarket
and I don't think taking Sienna and
Chloe to Hailey's house is a very

good idea, do you?"

Isla bit her lip. "No … but I promised. Hailey was really worried. I said I'd definitely go and check on the cats at lunchtime." She eyed Sienna and Chloe, who were both colouring at the kitchen table. Couldn't Mum just leave them for a few minutes? They were fine and it was only two doors down…

Except she wanted to spend longer than a few minutes fussing over both cats. And just then Sienna decided that Chloe's purple pen was nicer than hers and snatched it, and Chloe thought the best answer to that was to sweep all the pens off the table on to the floor…

So that wasn't happening.

"When Dad gets back from the supermarket," Isla's mum promised, hurrying to stop Sienna grabbing Chloe's drawing before she could rip it up.

"OK..." Isla sighed. Dad would be ages doing the big weekly shop and she'd told Hailey she'd absolutely, *definitely* go round at lunchtime.

Isla trailed out into the hallway and sat down on the stairs, where she could watch through the frosted glass in the front door for the car drawing up.

Sometimes she could really do without her little sisters.

After a few minutes sitting there with her chin on her hand, Isla realized that she was staring vaguely

at the big
key hanging
on the wall
beside the
front door.
It had a
row of little
hooks on it,
and it was where
her mum and dad
hung up their door keys, and any
other keys they had, like the spare key
for her nan's house – and the key to
Hailey's front door.

It was just there, right in front of
her.

And it would be helpful if she went
by herself, wouldn't it? Mum and Dad
were both busy, so why give them the

bother of having to go with her?

By this time, Isla had almost convinced herself that it was her duty to go, right now. Chloe and Sienna having another meltdown in the kitchen – because Sienna had tried to write her name and written the S the wrong way round – only made the decision even easier.

The kitten crouched in the darkness behind a basket of scarves and mittens. The house felt so strange without any of the family there. It creaked and echoed, and Silky's tail twitched. They had all been out before, but prhaps only for a few moments, or when she'd still been kept in one room by herself. This felt different.

She didn't know where Pickle was. The fur along her spine kept lifting every time she heard a noise and wondered if it was him, getting ready to leap out at her and cuff her with one of his massive paws.

A sharp rattling made her ears prick up. The sound of a key in the door. Perhaps the family had come back? Silky stood up, edging out from behind her basket and padding hopefully towards the line of pale light that was the door to the cupboard. This cupboard under the stairs was usually kept shut, but when she had finally made it to the bottom of the stairs Silky had seen that it was ajar and sneaked in. It was dark and quiet and it felt safe. Safe places were important now.

She peered round the edge of the cupboard, watching as the front door swung open. She expected to see Hailey run in but it was a different child. Different but familiar. She had met Isla before, though always with Hailey. What was the girl doing here?

Perhaps she wouldn't come out, not yet, Silky thought. She'd just watch.

"Silky! Pickle!" Isla called, her voice low. Silky knew her name but she didn't always answer to it, not unless it was someone calling her for food. She squished herself a little closer to the door of the cupboard, her whiskers quivering as she watched Isla. The girl was pulling something out of her pocket – it looked like a bundle of string and ribbons. And it bounced!

Without even thinking about it, Silky darted out from behind the cupboard door. The ribbons danced and sparkled and she wanted them. She heard Isla laugh and say, "Oh, there you are!" but the kitten wasn't listening. She was sitting up on her hind paws, batting at the dangling ribbons.

"Do you like them? I put them on
elastic so they'd jump about. I got it out of
Mum's basket of sewing stuff. Oooooh,
you caught it! Wow, big jump, Silky."

Silky leaped up again, flailing her
paws at the ribbons as they flashed
past her nose. She landed on the hall
carpet with a thump, the ball of ribbons
squashed underneath her, and she rolled
around with it, growling fiercely and
chewing at the bright strands.

"Do you like it then?" Isla crouched
down next to her and Silky could hear
the warmth in her voice. "I made it for
you. For Pickle too, but mostly you.
Hailey says Pickle's not that interested
in toys any more."

Silky rolled on to her back, still
clutching the fluffy ball of ribbons, and

rubbed the side of her head against Isla's outstretched hand. This was good. She liked being fussed over.

Isla laughed in delight and tickled under the kitten's chin. "You're so soft," she murmured. "Such long fur. I should have asked Hailey if I ought to brush you. Do you like being brushed, mmm?" She smoothed her hand over the kitten's fur. Silky was the perfect name for her.

There was a soft click from the kitchen – so quiet that Isla hardly even noticed it. But Silky sprang up at once, twisting back on to her paws and standing ready, shoulders hunched. Her fluffy tail seemed to get even fluffier and Isla saw her turn sideways. She was making herself look bigger, Isla realized, looking worriedly towards the kitchen.

Isla had never been afraid of Pickle
– even though he was really big. He
was such a friendly cat, and cuddly, and
she'd never seen him scratch anyone.

Now, stalking in from the kitchen, he
looked very different. He'd lowered his
head and his ears were flattened. The fur
along his back had lifted up in spikes and
he was hissing, no, more than hissing –
it was a deep, throaty growl. He seemed
about six times the size of Silky. He
looked *terrifying*.

"Pickle, no…" Isla said helplessly, wondering what she ought to do. She couldn't pick him up, not if he didn't want her to, not with only one hand. She could probably pick up Silky, though, since she was so small. But, before she could grab Silky out of Pickle's way, the big cat had surged forwards and smacked the kitten hard with a clawed paw.

Silky squeaked, rolling over out of his way. She hissed, trying to sound fierce, but she was so tiny it was obvious that she couldn't really fight back.

"Stop it!" Isla yelled as Pickle went to whack the little kitten again. "No! Bad cat, leave her alone!"

Pickle hardly seemed to notice.

Isla jumped in between them and tried to flap her hand to shoo him away. Pickle hissed again, furious, and darted round Isla. But Silky had taken her chance and shot back into the cupboard under the stairs.

Isla slammed the door shut before Pickle could get in there after her – she couldn't imagine trying to break up a cat fight inside a cupboard. It would be awful!

She glared at Pickle. "I know you don't want her here," she told him, "but that was just mean! She's tiny! How could you be so horrible?"

Pickle ignored her. He went to sniff at the cupboard door, growling very quietly, almost as though he was saying nasty things under his breath.

"Now what do I do?" Isla muttered, eyeing him anxiously. She was only supposed to be here for a few minutes to check up on them. Mum and Dad didn't even know where she was! But she couldn't leave the two cats like this, with Silky shut in a cupboard and Pickle on the warpath.

She was stuck.

Chapter Six

At that moment, the front door bell rang, followed by a loud knocking on the door. Isla bit her lip. She was pretty sure she knew who that was. She hurried to open the door and found her mum on the doorstep, looking panicked.

"Isla! You... I don't know what to say! I didn't know where you'd gone!"

Her mum suddenly hugged her so tightly that Isla squeaked. "Don't you *ever* do that again! We couldn't find you, and then I realized the key had gone. How could you just disappear? I told you I'd come with you as soon as Dad was back."

"I promised Hailey," Isla said, her voice muffled in her mum's T-shirt. "I said I'd go at lunchtime and we'd already had lunch. It was nearly two o'clock, Mum!" She pulled away from the hug. "And I was right to be worried. The cats just had a massive fight. It was awful."

"Silky and Pickle?" Isla's mum looked around and saw Pickle sitting by the cupboard door, eyeing her curiously. "Oh no, are they OK? Pickle looks all right. Where's Silky?"

"In the cupboard! Pickle was attacking her and she ran in there, so I shut the door to keep him away. But what do we do now?"

"Oh, Pickle..." Isla's mum looked thoughtful. "Perhaps we could put him in the kitchen. Has he got somewhere comfy to sleep in there?"

Isla nodded. "His bed's by the radiator. And he'd be able to go out through the cat flap – I think he'd really hate being shut in the house.

Silky's not been going out all that long. She probably won't mind so much."

"Yes, and it's only until they all come back tomorrow." Isla's mum sighed. "Julie said that she thought the cats were starting to settle down together. I hope we're doing the right thing splitting them up."

"You didn't see Pickle, Mum. He was so angry!" Isla assured her. "It might be OK if there was someone here to keep an eye on them, but not when they're on their own."

"I know. Don't worry, Isla. It's for the best. He still looks upset now. Pickle…" Isla's mum crouched down and called to him. "Come on, sweetie. Leave the kitten alone."

Pickle looked at her but he didn't

move, and Isla's mum sighed. "I hope he's not going to scratch," she murmured.

"He wouldn't!" Isla said, trying to sound reassuring. "He's a nice cat…"

Isla's mum scooped Pickle up gently, supporting him underneath, the same way Hailey did. Isla was a bit surprised – she hadn't realized that her mum knew how to look after a cat. Pickle looked quite surprised too, but he didn't scratch or hiss. He let Isla's mum shut him up in the kitchen without complaining.

As soon as the kitchen door was closed, Isla opened the cupboard under the stairs. She was expecting Silky to pop out at once but there was no sign of the kitten. Isla crouched down to peer inside. She didn't put the light on in case it scared the little cat, but she could sort of see in the light from the hallway.

"Is she all right?" Isla's mum said.

"I can't see her… Oh! There she is, behind the basket. The poor thing's shaking…" Isla crawled into the cupboard a little way and picked up the kitten, cuddling Silky against her front. She felt so small, like a shivery little bundle of bones and fur. "Do we have to go back home just yet?" Isla asked her mum. "I don't want to leave her like this."

"No, we can stay a bit longer. Chloe and Sienna are helping Dad put the shopping away – you know they like that." Her mum kneeled down beside Isla and looked anxiously at the kitten. "She's not hurt, is she?"

"No, I think she's just scared." Isla could feel Silky's heartbeat thudding against her fingers. The three of them sat quietly, Isla gently stroking Silky and her mum leaning against the wall, watching.

"You're very good with her," Isla's mum said after a little while. "She looks like she's calming down a bit."

"So were you! I mean with Pickle, the way you picked him up. You knew just how to hold him."

"I like cats," her mum said, smiling. "We used to have a lovely big black cat like Pickle when I was growing up. He was called Oliver." She reached over and gently stroked the top of Silky's head with one finger. "Isla, would you like us to get a cat?"

Isla stared at her. "You know I would!" she said at last. "I've asked and asked, but you always said no because of Sienna and Chloe."

"I think they're nearly old enough to be sensible with one now," her mum said. "They're starting school in September. They're getting big."

"Would Dad like us to have a cat?" Isla said.

"Mmmm, well, I talked to him about it and he wasn't totally sure, but he said maybe." Her mum smiled. "I reckon we could convince him. Perhaps we could go to the same shelter that Hailey and her family got Silky from. What do you think?"

"That would be amazing…" Isla smiled up at her.

But deep inside there was a tiny sad thought – *if only Mum had said that a few weeks ago! We could have been the ones to adopt Silky. She would be living with us and not having to hide from Pickle…*

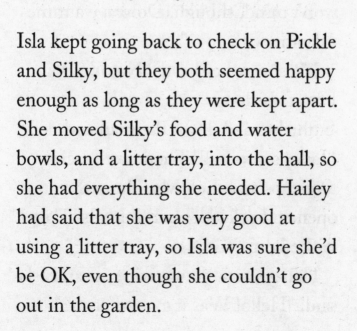

Isla kept going back to check on Pickle and Silky, but they both seemed happy enough as long as they were kept apart. She moved Silky's food and water bowls, and a litter tray, into the hall, so she had everything she needed. Hailey had said that she was very good at using a litter tray, so Isla was sure she'd be OK, even though she couldn't go out in the garden.

Isla just hoped Hailey's mum and dad wouldn't mind. She kept an eye out for their car on Sunday afternoon, checking to see if it was in the driveway, and as soon she spotted it, she asked her dad if it was OK to pop round and explain.

"Of course you can. I'm sure they won't mind, though. Do you want me to come with you?"

Isla shook her head. "No, it's OK. I won't be long."

She hurried down the road and rang Hailey's doorbell. There were racing footsteps and then Max flung the door open and yelled, "Hailey! It's Isla!" and dashed off again.

Hailey came down the stairs and Isla said, "Hello! Was it a good party?"

"It was really good, I stayed up till half past one!"

Hailey looked tired, though, Isla thought. She was very pale and there were dark shadows under her eyes. "Wow! Lucky! Um, I just wanted to explain about the cats being in separate rooms."

Hailey looked surprised. "I hadn't noticed. Although Mum did mention that Silky's bowls had been moved into the hallway."

"Pickle and Silky had a big fight on Saturday – he chased her into the cupboard under the stairs and I was really worried, so me and Mum put the litter tray and bowls out in the hall for Silky, and shut Pickle in the kitchen. I hope that's OK?"

Hailey nodded. "Thanks, Isla. But I'm sure they would have been all right," she added.

Isla bit her lip. She didn't think so. "You didn't see Pickle," she said slowly. "He was so angry with Silky. It was scary."

"Pickle's not scary!" Hailey said indignantly. "He's a lovely cat."

"Yes, I know… But…"

"But what?" Hailey snapped.

Isla didn't know what to say. She knew Hailey adored Pickle and hated to think that he was fierce, but Silky had been so terrified. She felt as though she had to stick up for the little kitten. "But Pickle really hates sharing his house. *You* were the one who told *me* that!"

"And I said he'll get used to it!" Hailey was suddenly yelling. "It's none of your business anyway. Pickle's my cat, and so's Silky! You should just keep your nose out of it! I wish I'd never let you come and look after them!"

Isla felt hot and prickly all over. Hailey looked so angry – her fists were clenched and there were red spots on her cheeks. Isla didn't think she'd ever seen her like that before.

She made a sort of stifled gasping

noise and then turned and ran back down the street towards her house. She'd left the front door on the latch so she just pushed it open and then raced inside, flinging herself down on a beanbag in the living room. She couldn't stop crying.

Chapter Seven

Silky cowered back against the bottom
step of the stairs. She hated shouting
almost as much as she hated Pickle's
scary hissing noises. Usually she loved
being around Hailey and Isla. They were
so gentle, and they'd spend ages fussing
over her and playing with her and
feeding her cat treats. But now she could
feel the anger buzzing between them

and it was setting her whiskers tingling.

She watched Isla stumble down the path and then Hailey turned away from the door and buried her face in the coats hanging from hooks on the wall. Her shoulders were heaving. Silky eyed her for a moment and then slipped out of the open door into the front garden. She could hear Isla's footsteps on the pavement and she darted after her. She peered round the edge of Isla's front wall just in time to see the door slam as Isla ran inside.

Silky looked back along the street, wondering what to do. Right now, she didn't want to go back to Hailey's house. Pickle was there, and so was Hailey, and at the moment Hailey just made her think scary and loud.

Isla, though – Isla had rescued her from Pickle and then held her so gently, stroking her and whispering until Silky's heart had stopped hammering inside her. Silky padded into Isla's garden, stepping carefully over the crunchy gravel, and looked thoughtfully at the door. There was no way in there but there was a little path round the side of the house.

Silky went to investigate, pressed close against the wall, tail held low. She wasn't sure if there was another cat here, ready to jump out at her. She made it all the way to a small, sunny garden and her ears pricked forwards. The sunny patches looked so inviting and there was a butterfly swooping low over the grass. Silky forgot about Isla and Hailey and the shouting, and dashed after it, making a ballet-dancer leap in the middle of the lawn. But the butterfly twirled away over the fence, leaving the small kitten far below.

Silky shook her whiskers crossly and then stopped dead still, staring at the house. The back door was open and there were good smells coming out. Perhaps Isla was in there and would make a fuss of her like she had the day before.

The back door led into the kitchen, which Silky thought was empty – it was certainly very quiet. Cautiously, she pattered up to the back step and hopped inside. She stood there, eyes wide and ears swivelling. She froze as someone began to whistle quietly on the far side of the kitchen – Isla's dad was making dinner. But he was looking down at the vegetables he was chopping and didn't see a small, striped kitten pad quietly across the room and into the hallway.

There Silky stood, looking around uncertainly. She could go upstairs but that would take a lot of effort. She knew about stairs and she much

preferred to have someone carry her
up and down. Otherwise
there were a couple
of doors she could
try. One sounded
rather noisy –
she could hear
giggling and
banging and
some sort of
squeaky toy –
and she wasn't
sure about that
at all. The other
room was quieter.
But as she stood there,
listening, she caught a strange hiccupy
sort of noise, muffled and sad.

What was it?

Silky crept round the living-room door and saw Isla, half sitting, half lying, on a big beanbag. Her face was buried against her arm and she was crying quietly into the soft cover of the beanbag.

Silky stood watching her for a moment and then jumped on to the sofa – she liked to be high up and looking down, it made her feel safer. She walked along until she was just next to Isla on the beanbag and then she mewed.

Isla didn't notice – or didn't seem to at first. Then the heaving gasps she was making stopped and she turned to look round at the sofa. Silky gazed back hopefully and Isla laughed. "Silky? What are you doing here?"

Isla sat up, wriggling round on the beanbag. "Did you follow me home?" she asked the kitten. She rubbed Silky's ears and smiled as the tabby kitten began to purr. "I should take you back," she murmured. "Hailey won't know where you are." But then she shivered. She didn't want to go back to Hailey's, not just yet.

Slowly, so as not to scare the kitten, Isla got up from the beanbag and sat down next to Silky on the sofa. She stroked her ears again and then ran her hand gently all the way down Silky's back. The purring grew louder.

"You're nearly shaking with purrs," Isla said, starting to laugh. "I don't know how someone as little as you can make that much noise."

Silky marched firmly up on to Isla's lap and stomped round in a circle, as though she was trying to knead Isla's legs like dough. Clearly she wanted them just the right shape for a kitten. Then she curled herself into a tiny striped ball and yawned.

"Oh… You shouldn't go to sleep," Isla said. "I have to take you back." But she didn't say it very loudly.

"What's that?" a small voice said, and Isla started. Sienna was standing by the arm of the sofa, staring down at the kitten in Isla's lap. Within seconds, Chloe had appeared too and the pair of them gazed accusingly at Isla.

"You got a cat!"

"Is that your cat, Isla?"

"No," Isla whispered sadly. "She's Hailey's. Do you remember me telling you about her? She's called Silky. I think she must have followed me home. I have to take her back in a minute."

"I want to stroke her!" Sienna announced, and Chloe chimed in, "And me!"

Isla looked at them worriedly. Silky was so tiny … and Sienna and Chloe could be rough sometimes. But then Mum had said she thought they were maybe old enough to get a cat and

Silky didn't seem to be scared of them. She'd given up on sleeping and was now standing up in Isla's lap, gazing curiously at the two small girls.

"You can stroke her," Isla said. "But you have to be really, really gentle. You mustn't hurt her or scare her, OK?"

"Yes!" Chloe said, bouncing on to the sofa beside Isla.

"I want to be next to the kitten," Sienna demanded. "It was me said first!"

Isla wriggled so there was space either side of her, hoping that Silky wouldn't get fed up and leap away. But she just balanced like a little kitten surfer. "There, now there's room for you both," Isla said. "You can stroke her but you have to take turns," she added hurriedly. "And not too hard on her head."

"She's soft," Chloe whispered.

"Softer than a teddy," Sienna agreed. "So soft."

Isla watched, surprised, as Chloe and Sienna took turns stroking, each one waiting patiently. She hadn't expected them to be so good. "You can tickle her under the chin too," she suggested, showing them what she meant. "She likes that. Listen, can you hear her purring?"

"Like a car!" Chloe said, giggling.

"Yeah, or the lawnmower," Isla agreed. Then a tiny noise from the doorway made her look up and she realized that her dad was standing there, watching them. Isla looked down at the kitten in her lap, eyes closed and purring with delight, and wondered how she was going to explain.

"So why do we have a cat?" her dad asked, coming to sit down next to Chloe.

"She's Hailey's," Chloe told him. "Her name's Silky. Isn't she nice, Daddy?"

"Very nice," he agreed. "But why is she *here*?"

"I think she followed me home,"

Isla said. "Honestly, Dad, I didn't bring her with me on purpose. I was in here and then I just looked up and Silky was on the sofa staring at me! I don't even know how she got in." Then she sighed. "I was just about to take her back."

"Aww, not yet. Can't we stroke her a little bit more?" Sienna pleaded. "We're being good like you said."

"You really are," their dad murmured, watching them with his eyebrows raised. "You're being very good. Well done, Isla." Then he added, "Can I have a go?"

"You have to take turns," Chloe told him sternly. "Like we are. Tickle under her chin like this, Daddy."

"Wow, she likes that, doesn't she?"

Their dad laughed as Silky suddenly began to purr louder. Then she stood up and gave a stretch that arched her back and made her almost twice as tall. She looked around thoughtfully and marched straight over Chloe's lap and on to Dad's. She sat down again, padded thoughtfully at his trousers and then collapsed over on to her side, showing off her white spotted tummy.

Dad shook his head. "Well, she knows which side her bread's buttered," he murmured, cautiously scratching Silky's tummy fur with one finger.

Chloe and Sienna scrambled round him on the sofa so they could snuggle up close and pet the kitten too. Isla watched them, smiling sadly.

Mum had said that they needed to convince Dad about getting a cat. She reckoned Silky might just have done it for them.

Chapter Eight

Isla glanced up – was that a knocking on the door? It was very faint. Dad had told her that Mum had gone out for a run, so Isla decided she'd better answer it. When she opened the door, Hailey was standing on the step, her face blotchy and tear-stained.

"Oh!" Isla didn't know what else to say. She just stared at Hailey, hoping

that she wasn't going to yell again.
And how was she going to explain that
Silky was in her living room?

"I came to say I'm sorry," Hailey
said. She sounded sniffly. "I should
never have shouted at you and I know
you were only worried about Silky."

"It's OK—" Isla started to say, but
Hailey hadn't finished.

"I think I only got upset because I
knew you were right." She glanced up
at Isla. "My mum
said the same
thing in the car
on the way home.
That she was
really worried
about Pickle and
she wasn't sure he

was ever going to be able to cope with another cat living in his house. That we have to take Silky back. She said Pickle seems sad all the time and she's sure he isn't eating as much. Mum thinks he's even lost weight!"

"Oh wow…"

Hailey sighed. "At least the vet will be pleased. She said he was getting a bit fat. But Silky's not happy either. I know that really. She hides all the time because she's scared of Pickle. We can't even find her right now. She's so tiny she can squeeze herself into all these little spaces and we don't have a clue where she's got to."

"Um, actually I was just about to come and see you." Isla gave an apologetic shrug. "I know where Silky is."

Hailey looked relieved. "Is she OK?"

"Come and see." Isla led Hailey down the hallway to the living room. "You have to be quiet…" she whispered, pointing through the door.

There on the sofa were Dad, Chloe and Sienna, all fast asleep. Isla's dad was slumped against the back of the sofa, making tiny snoring noises. Sienna and Chloe were curled up halfway across his lap, and between them was Silky, adding her own purry little snores to the mix. The tabby kitten was on her back, and she'd slumped slightly into the gap between Isla's dad's legs. All her paws were in the air and it made them look massive. She was so funny that Isla had to smile, even though she was worried about what Hailey was going to say.

"I was going to bring her back to you," Isla whispered. "But then I realized they'd all gone to sleep, so I thought I'd wait till they woke up. My mum's gone for a run and Dad's supposed to be making dinner, so it wouldn't have been much longer. Sorry… Hey, don't cry!" She put her arm round Hailey's shoulders. "It's all right. Silky's OK. I'm sorry, I should have brought her back straight away."

"It isn't that," Hailey sniffed, and then pulled Isla gently out into the hallway. "I'm only crying because she looks so sweet."

Isla shook her head, not understanding.

"She's so lovely and I don't want her to go back to the shelter," Hailey explained. "She'll be all on her own in one of those pens and she'll hate it. I know they're brilliant at looking after the animals but it's not like having a real home." More tears ran down her cheeks. "She might even like the shelter better than our house because she's been so scared and that makes me feel *awful*!"

"She knows you love her," Isla said, giving Hailey a hug. "It's only Pickle she doesn't like. Do you really have to take her back there?"

Hailey nodded. "I told Mum what happened yesterday and that made up her mind. We have to let Silky go because it's not fair on either of them. There's going to be times when there's no one in the house to make sure they aren't fighting and we can't always keep them separated. It just won't work so we have to send her back." Hailey gave a shuddery sort of sigh. "I'm almost looking forward to it. Poor Pickle, he's been so miserable. At least he'll be happy again."

"I know you'll really miss her, but Silky won't be at the shelter for long,"

Isla said, trying to look on the bright side. "She's so gorgeous, someone's going to adopt her straight away."

"Do you think so?" Hailey asked hopefully. "There were so many cats there, Isla. It was really sad."

There was a rustling from inside the living room and Isla's dad appeared at the door with a sleepy Silky cradled in his cupped hands. "I think this might be yours," he said to Hailey, holding out the kitten. Silky gave a huge yawn and blinked at Hailey.

"Yeah…" Hailey took Silky and cuddled her close. "I'd better take her home." She sighed. "For now, anyway."

"What's up?" Isla's dad looked

between the two girls, eyebrows raised.

"They've decided that Silky's got to go back to the shelter," Isla told him. "Pickle hates sharing his house."

"Max is already asking if we can have a tortoise instead…" Hailey said, rolling her eyes. "He reckons Pickle won't mind a tortoise. Max thinks he might even ride on it – he's seen a video of a cat riding a tortoise." She smiled at Isla and her dad. "Thanks for looking after Silky so well. I wish you could keep her instead."

Isla caught her breath. She hadn't thought of it – she couldn't believe she hadn't thought of it. Mum had said she'd like to have a cat if they could persuade Dad. And Dad had just told her and Sienna and Chloe how good they all were with Silky. He'd had Silky curled up on his lap asleep for ages, like a born cat owner! She stared at him pleadingly.

"Well..." Isla's dad looked at Silky, who was climbing on to Hailey's shoulder and sniffing at her hair. "I suppose we could think about it. I mean, we'd have to talk to your mum, Isla. Your parents too, Hailey. And I'm not sure what the shelter would say about Silky swapping owners..."

"They'd be glad Silky's got a new home, Dad. I'm sure they would!" Isla felt like jumping up and down. Was he actually saying yes?

"Can we?" she whispered. "Please can we?"

"I'm not promising," Isla's dad said slowly. "But … I don't see why she has to go back to the shelter to be honest. I should think it would be upsetting for her. She'd be better off staying with us."

Hailey swallowed hard and carefully unwound Silky from her hair. She handed her over to Isla, and Isla could see that she was trying not to cry again.

"You'll be able to see her all the

time," she said quietly. "She'll still be a bit yours. We can share her."

Silky was settling into the crook of Isla's elbow, as though she was meant to be there. She yawned again and Isla leaned down and rubbed her chin over the top of Silky's head, loving the velvet feel of her fur.

"I've got Pickle," Hailey said. "I expect he'll sleep on my bed tonight."

Isla nodded and tried not to look too happy, but it was hard. She was imagining Silky sleeping on hers.

Out Now

The Mystery Kitten

From best-selling author
HOLLY WEBB

Illustrated by Sophy Williams